PLEASE DO NOT FEED THE ANIMALS

ZOO DREAMS

COR HAZELAAR

Frances Foster Books

Farrar Straus Giroux

New York

For Nanny and Pops

Library of Congress Cataloging-in-Publication Data.
Hazelaar, Cor.
Zoo dreams / Cor Hazelaar. — 1st ed. "Frances Foster Books."
p.   cm.
[1. Zoo animals—Fiction. 2. Zoos—Fiction. 3. Sleep—Fiction.]
I. Title. PZ7. H3149674Zo 1997   [E]—dc20   96-19438 CIP

After the last visitor has left, the zookeepers begin their nightly rounds.

Most of the animals sleep indoors. Some sleep
standing, like the elegant giraffes.

The zookeepers watch the penguins hop out of their icy pool and settle down for the night. A few have fuzzy babies hidden among the rocks.

The snow monkeys finish their dinner and their games, and pile together in groups of family and friends.

The polar bear curls up like a big cat.

Are the crocodiles asleep? And the turtles?

Perched on viny branches, the toucans doze.

The fish sleep with their eyes open! They drift slowly in the dark tanks.

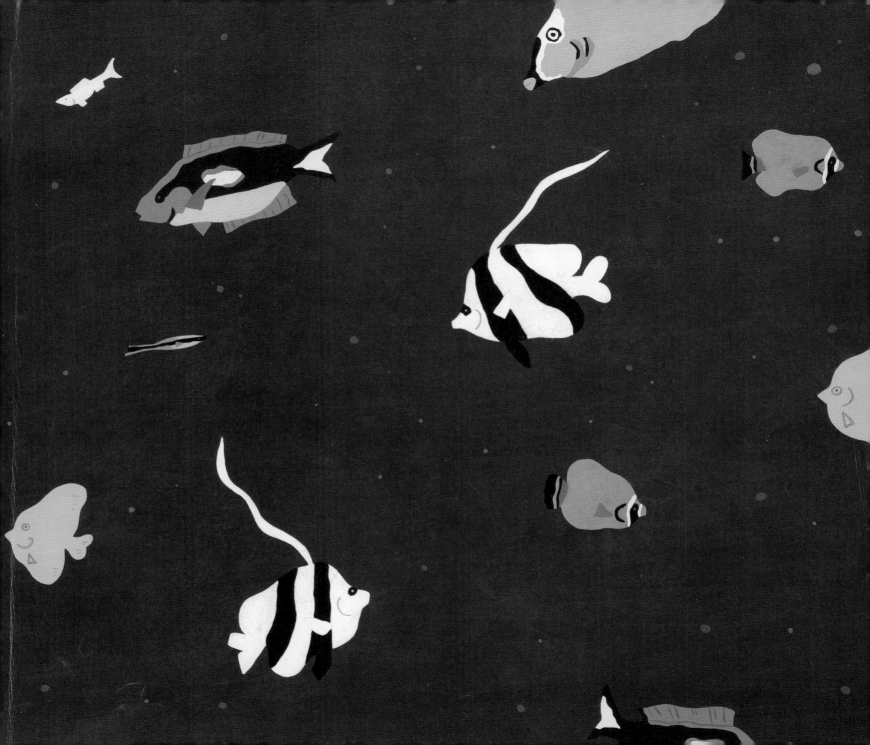

The zookeepers switch on the lights in the bats'
cave. This tricks them into sleeping at night. Bats
in the wild fly around at night and sleep by day.

The sea lions couldn't be cozier, stretched out
on their damp and rocky bed.

Satisfied that all the animals are comfortable and
fed, the zookeepers head for home.

. . . and finally to bed, to dream zoo dreams.